Other Lives

Other Lives

ISBN: 978-1986024341

.

Cover photo: Dede Reed
Book design: Dede Reed

Printed in the United States of America

Plaindealing Press
P.O. Box 156
Royal Oak, Maryland

Contents

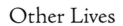

Other Lives

"We close at six. You have not much time," a man in the *fundación* office said in faltering English. He handed Paula a pamphlet and put her five pesos in a drawer. "To see the ruins, go on that street." He nodded toward an alleyway between the colonial buildings.

Although Paula heard sounds of tools in the distance where digging had been going on in a newly discovered pre-Columbian site, the rest of the historic neighborhood was quiet. She was not interested in the excavation, in clay pots shaped like frogs or vessels used for grain portage; she wanted to visit the colonial houses—be surrounded by thick stone walls and waxed furniture and hear water in fountains. She cared about the history of dust, of abandoned lives—stoneware in a cupboard, a clock stopped in a long-ago past.

Paula had walked across Guanajuato through the hottest part of the afternoon. Distances for her were important; they were a part of her journey, part of the process of arriving, of being somewhere. During the past two months in Mexico, she had traveled on buses, walked beaches, visited Indian villages, and wandered all around Mexico City—for entire days sometimes. Perhaps, after she visited the neighboring city of San Miguel, she would go back to Richmond, but for now, she thought only about the day at hand—what she was going to see, where she would eat and sleep.

This afternoon Paula was worn out. She had walked past mechanic shops, ceramic studios and tortilla factories. She took refuge in a plaza and dozed for a moment, and when she woke up, she considered going back to her hotel to lie down but remembered the historic houses in the old part of town.

Now, with a ticket stub in hand, she stood outside an ochre-colored house with high iron gates and read in her brochure that the Prieto family had left in 1926, during the Cristero war—set off by religious persecution of the Catholics. In this house she would see crucifixes, carved saints and paintings of Madonnas. Weary of religious icons, she sat on a bench to read about the other houses she might be interested in looking at, and sipped her bottle of water. The taste was stale.

"Hola?"

Though Paula did not know anyone, had not really had significant conversations since she had begun the trip, she looked up.

"Señorita?"

It was a voice she almost recognized, recently heard; it was neither pushy nor reticent, friendly nor desperate. She looked around and noticed a man near her in the street.

"You mean me?"

He was standing in the shade squarely on his feet, hands in his pockets—the left one jiggling a clinking noise—and he wore a smile that she couldn't quite read.

He was watching her, seemed to have time on his hands. He wasn't a tourist.

"Are you talking to me?" She pointed to herself. She was flushed; sweat had soaked her back. It occurred to her how this

Mexican sun was getting to her: its heat sapping her fluids as if needing to absorb them back to feed the dried out ruins of the pre-Columbian site or the crumbling plaster of the colonial houses. Oddly, now that she thought about it, it was water that attracted her here. She'd read how in the 1500s Guanajuato was built over a river; the flow was channeled under the city in a maze of tunnels. Now the wider tunnels carried the traffic here, and the smaller ones, pedestrians there; the river had been rerouted in three canals. The Fundación de Casas Históricas was restoring a block of seventeenth-century houses along the river.

The man stepped out of the shadow and walked to her. He threw his arms in the air as if he knew her and was surprised to somehow find her there. He seemed familiar; he had a particular look in his eyes, a glimmer. His smile tested her, invited her—it widened, relaxed, widened again. He tilted his head. He remained quiet, just stood there, but he didn't make her nervous. She noticed he was wearing a blazer.

"You come with?" he said, as if picking his words from a limited vocabulary. "You can see someplace special."

He began to walk away, his shoes clicked on the cobblestone. He stopped and looked back. "You come, no?"

He appeared surprised that she had not gotten up, that she was still on the bench, with her legs crossed and her water bottle in hand. "Hurry, hurry," he said. "We have not all day."

Though Paula had no intention of budging, she found herself smiling.

"What is your name?" she asked.

He walked back but did not show in his face any sense of success. "My name is Juventino. In English, it is Young. My father and his father were in *Inglaterra*. My father changed back to Juventino when he came home to Mexico in the '70s. The names are not really the same. My first name is Francisco, but I am called Juventino anyway. It does not make sense two languages, two names."

Paula looked at him. He radiated optimism, innocence, a tinge of sophistication. "I can't come," she said, "it's late. I've time to see only one house." She was wary of Latino men, their intentions.

Not ready to give up, Juventino reached into his pocket and produced a ring of keys. "I have special entrance. No one else can see this *residencia*. It is not open to public."

Paula then recognized that he was one of the men in the *fundación* office. She was tempted, yet knew better. But before thinking further she said, "Okay, but just a tour. *Correcto?*"

"I am *hombre correcto*. I just show you a *residencia* you will like. I notice you take time to look."

They walked down the cobblestone street away from the balconied houses, away from the shops and plaza, the theatre and the walls of a cemetery, down a curving street until they came to a narrow tunnel. Juventino took Paula's hand.

"I lead you through here. It is dark. I am knowing the way."

Paula tensed as his fingers curled around hers, she was ready to pull back, turn around, but his hand was cool, like the shade they had just stepped into and he held her hand firmly, as if to protect her. Juventino was not tall, but he was taller than Paula. He had to duck slightly under the passageway. On the other side, he dropped her hand and walked next to her, but then, as if in a hurry, he picked up his pace. She had to scurry to keep up so she wouldn't lose him as he turned down an alley, went up a stairway and then went down another street. He stopped when they came to a stream, what had been the river—but was now just a trickle of water—and waited before he led her to a door of a large stone house.

Juventino fiddled with the keys, found the one he needed and turned the lock. He leaned against the door; it was heavy, but once he budged it from the sill, it swung open slowly. He took Paula's arm and guided her into a hall.

"*Aquí!*" he said. "A *casa colonial.*" He swooped his arm back as if he had been the first to discover it.

"Whose house is it?" Paula was standing in a pool of light. The last rays of afternoon sun streamed in through high windows.

"The *familia* Cayetano lived here. Early eighteenth century. It is *matriarcal*—passed down through women. Now it is at the end of the line and has been left to the *fundación*. Come, come." He led her from room to room, pointing at the Spanish wood paneling in the halls, the terracotta pots hanging in the kitchen, blue tiles behind the stove. She noticed a shawl draped on a chair, toy soldiers on a shelf, stains in the porcelain tub, and from a balcony, overgrown banana trees.

"You like, no?" He smiled as she glanced up at the plaster arches and then peered out of windows to get views of the courtyard gardens.

"It is beautiful. Haunting even, like a house in a dream." Eyeing a crooked frame of an ink drawing on the wall, Paula reached to straighten it, but Juventino grabbed her hand.

"No touching," he said, "Treat like a museum."

Paula blushed, feeling suddenly childish, embarrassed, and began to pull her hand free of his, but he had already let go. Now, he put his other hand on her elbow and steered her back onto the upstairs landing and then down the steps. Once on the main floor, she followed him into a hall until they came to a door. He rattled the key ring until he found a long one. This time the door swung open as soon as he unlocked it.

"Now," he said whispering. "This part is *privada*. La señora died two years ago. She was old. No one can come here yet."

Juventino turned on a light. Gold lettering on hundreds of books lining an octagonal library sparkled. They stood in awe for a few moments in the comforting smell of old leather. He led her through the library out to a courtyard.

"Catarina was her first name. No one saw her for many years. Fifty maybe. She lived alone in this wing. You will see," Juventino said, motioning to her.

Unlike the neglected gardens around the rest of the house, everything in this courtyard was immaculate: thyme grew between the stones, amaryllis was blooming, the fountain bubbled.

"No shoes," Juventino said as he kicked off his loafers. "Put them here next to mine." But before she got her second sneaker off, he was on his knee, removing it from her foot. Paula blushed, pulled her foot back and said, "I can take it off."

"We must walk softly. Not scrape the wooden floors with heels." He shook his finger.

The rooms surrounding the courtyard all had outside doors, but inside they connected like a train. Here, in this wing, the rooms were smaller, the ceilings lower. It was like a cloister, Paula thought. A nunnery. No sounds of the street seeped through the walls. She expected, when she walked into the first room, to see religious artifacts, an altar or prayer chairs, but the walls were bleached white, and windows opened into the courtyard. There was a large painting in a gold frame on the wall.

"You are feeling it too?" Juventino commented after they had spent a few moments in a living room under a portrait of a young woman sitting in a chair in a garden. "She is seeing us, wherever we are, her eyes move." He stepped back and crossed his arms.

"But what you are feeling will not last. When the house is open for visitors, la Señora Catarina will not see any more. It is how it is when someplace is changed." He paused, scratched his head and added, "I have seen this in other restoration houses. *Los conservadores* spray the insects, they paint, they move furniture to the side, they clean with *cloro*. It is the same house, but not the same. The feeling leaves. There is no reminder where people sat to think. No reminder of music, of conversations. The paintings become just paint on canvas." He paused, looked sad, stricken almost, and then said, "Come, come, there is more."

Each of the rooms in the wing had portraits of Señora Catarina Cayetano. In one, she was sitting by a window; morning light lit her face. In another she was standing in a doorway in a long dress. In one room there was a small portrait of her looking at herself in a mirror, her hands shaping her hair into a bun. Paula moved around the room; the woman's eyes followed— they were alive, there was a presence. In all of the portraits the woman's mouth was parted, there was a slight smile, a suggestion of contentment. Yes, that was it, thought Paula. She had time; she was comfortable in herself.

"She *is* watching us."

Juventino patted Paula's back. "Yes," he said simply.

As they proceeded, Paula noticed that there were no portraits of the Señora as a middle-aged woman. She wondered what caused the painter to stop painting. Maybe he had died?

Juventino's hand on her shoulder startled her. She jumped, scared suddenly that something else—a wind, a ghostly weight—had touched her. She dropped her shoulder, his hand slid off.

"Something is strange," Paula said.

Juventino crossed the room and opened the door out to the courtyard. "You have intuition. These portraits were, after the incident, hidden in a back room. She did not want the remembering." He looked perplexed. He made the sign of the cross. Paula couldn't detect why. There was something else.

"What happened?"

Juventino picked up a dead branch that had caught behind the door when he opened it. Then, standing under the portal, he said, "She left a candle in her son's room. There began a fire. The child was saved, but Señora Catarina's face and her chest and her hair were burned beyond knowing. She suffered in hospital for months and months. Specialists came from Mexico City, from Havana also. She grew away from her family and became reclusive. After, she did not want to see anyone. There was a period when she cried, nothing else, just cried. She would not even be with her husband. He was a painter. She respected his love for beauty. The husband and son left for England, where he came from."

Paula's interest—her need to know the rest of the story—was a given. It was who she was at the bottom of her being. She had felt this urge before. Felt a sting in her eyes watching a young woman kiss her *novio* goodbye at the bus station in Oaxaca. There was the beggar woman, limping down the street, pushing a cart with all of her belongings. There was a memory of a man at a fountain in Pueblo—drunk—slapping water on his face. She knew, felt, that if she could just reach out to people, she might make a difference in their lives, she might make a difference in her life. She might find a way to belong. But, of course, she did not trespass into their sorrows. She was shy.

But now, she was sure that a small gesture would make a difference. She did not know what that could be.

"She means something to you," was all she could say. She watched how Juventino had shut his expressions down and pushed his emotions away.

He didn't answer. He looked away. Shook his head.

After a while he said, "She did not talk. Would not eat. Would not bathe.

"For years. She spent all her time reading. Escaping perhaps in her mind to other lives, other places. Later—years later—she began to tend to this garden. All day planting and weeding. A private shrine for her to beauty."

Paula remembered a dream from the night before—perhaps sparked from a woodcut she saw in a museum in Mexico City— of a medieval woman alone walking in a convent.

"Tell me more," Paula implored.

But Juventino was distracted. He picked a weed from the path. Skimmed a wilted water lily out of the fountain. Then he looked up at the failing afternoon light. Shade had spread itself into the valley of the river, into the garden.

Finally he said, "She decided to live only in this small part of the house. The servants never altered anything in the main *casa*. They were afraid to touch the happiness of the past. The life that was gone."

Paula pictured the young woman—now old—covered by black cloth walking at night, leaning on the arm of a maid.

"And she was so alone," Paula said feeling a chill, feeling sad and alone too. She rubbed her arms and said, "how do you know all of this?"

Juventino shrugged his shoulders as if he would say no more. As if he had said enough for one afternoon. He looked at his watch. "It is late. I have to return the keys to the office. I can show you more tomorrow."

He walked fast. His natural pace, Paula thought. They took the same route along the river, and then veered through the twisting streets. Paula was out of breath, but kept up. Juventino came to an alley and slowed down. They walked past shops closing, past a park where children were playing, a church with bells ringing. When they came to the dark pedestrian tunnel, she did not wait for him to offer her his hand; she slipped hers into his. As before, his palm was cool, like the shade they had just stepped into. He held her hand firmly in the dark tunnel, guiding her. When they got to the other side, she did not let go.

Pilar

Pilar Fuentes was standing in front of the window in a small turquoise room in a hotel in Veracruz, Mexico. The door had been left open. I knocked and waited. She turned and greeted me with a thin smile, hiding what I soon learned was loneliness and anguish.

In those days I worked as a refugee counselor for the Mexican Departamento de Relaciones de Refugiados. Pilar Fuentes was one of the first refugees I was to help. I was only twenty-five, had just finished a postgraduate degree at the Insituto Politénico Nacional in Mexico City and had hardly traveled abroad other than the United States, but from my studies of Latin American dictatorships, I had developed an interest in political dissidents. I was young, hankering to save the world, seething with righteousness, anxious to begin *my* work, while across the Caribbean Sea, Castro—in his army fatigues and scruffy beard—was arresting people for thinking.

Pilar was in her mid-forties, her salty-colored hair twisted into a braid. She was thin, wore a brown skirt that fell in loose pleats and a white blouse. She turned and looked at me after I mentioned my affiliation with the Relaciones de Refugiados— or she looked through me as if she could see the debutante I was, and, if I was the person who was going to make a difference in her life, she had been again defeated. I waited, nervous, but had my mission.

She came to the door, opened it all the way and said, *"Pase por favor,"* She then sat on the edge of the bed and indicated I should sit in the chair. She began to speak but then stopped, not sure, perhaps, to trust her thoughts. The room was tidy; a faint breeze rattled the aluminum blinds. Books and a few rolled canvases that she could fit into her suitcases were on the desk. Pilar attempted another smile and opened her mouth to speak. "I am here," she muttered, "where I never imagined to be." She enunciated each word slowly, her Cuban accent strong, distinctive.

Pilar was a widow, a painter, and wrote articles on the history of Cuban art. She told me how two years ago, she met Tomás Robertson, an Anglo-Argentine art dealer who'd come to Cuba to buy art. She'd been his guide. They'd had a short romance. He'd get her a job, he wrote later, he'd help her set up a studio if ever she could leave. Her husband, a professor in the department of political science, had been imprisoned in the early years of the Castro regime and died of typhoid fever. She had been in detention camps twice for her so-called anti-communist associations.

Now, she was determined to go to Argentina.

During the few weeks when Cubans were allowed to leave in the Mariel boatlift, Pilar—from one moment to the next—decided to go. She left her friends, her dingy apartment and took a bus to the coast. By the time she got to the port of Mariel, the only boat she could get on was going to Mexico. Now that she was here, I was to help her apply for immigration, but as I sat on the chair, the weight of her displacement made me sad.

"I no longer know how to think about life," she said.

I had learned about the remorse refugees suffer; it was set in her face, in the effort it took for her to speak without faltering.

We sat for a while in her room. I shuffled in my satchel of forms to fill the awkward moments. Then she said, "I cannot look at paperwork. I cannot concentrate to read."

"Let's take a walk," I suggested. I wondered if she'd been out at all since she had arrived two days earlier. We wandered along the Avila Camacho; the sun burned the pavement, harbor water sloshed against the sea wall. We soon found ourselves ducking into the arcades for shade. I asked about the trip.

"The waves splashed on deck," she said. "I was dizzy, could not eat, could not stay below. I did not know anyone, did not want to talk."

"Can I help you find family members who've immigrated?"

"No, she said," I have no family anywhere, anymore; they are gone; died or killed years ago."

People on the street looked at her—her worn leather purse slung around her neck like a sling of a gun. No one in Veracruz wore dark clothes or heavy shoes or had such a severe expression. I regretted offering to walk, but she seemed to like being out and kept looking eastward over the water, in the direction of Cuba.

We walked for half an hour and then stopped for lemonade. After I ordered, she looked at me and said, "I need to learn English. My Argentine friend's family is English. He sells art to the English and the Americans."

I offered myself as a teacher; my grandmother was American. Pilar fretted that she was too old to learn how to speak another language, but since she was in Veracruz for the time being (with dollars her parents had saved), she forced herself to try.

After her first week in the hotel, I helped her move her two suitcases into a building with a view of the water.

Soon she revealed another layer. Before she left Cuba she had not heard from Tomás for four months. All at once, his letters had stopped coming, but in the last one, he had warned her that he had to lay low for a while; the Argentine military government was arresting and killing writers and intellectuals; they were suspicious of his travels to Cuba and Bolivia.

"I cannot make English words stay in my mind. They dissolve as I try to memorize them," Pilar said after our second or third lesson. I tried to console her, to tell her that learning a language took time and felt like water seeping through sand, and the sand was drying quickly, but she shook her head. "No, it is not like that. I am a child when I speak English. I do not have strong words, just infantile ones. I will never be able to speak of feelings."

I encouraged her to apply for permanent residency in Mexico so that at least, as she was waiting to locate the whereabouts of Tomás, she'd feel as if she belonged someplace, but she could not make that decision, could not see a reason to settle permanently here. She, like all refugees, had lost a part of herself by losing her country but in her case it was not just recently, not a result of having gotten into a boat and motored away—this loss had been eating away at her every day in small indelible ways for twenty years.

We worked hard on the lessons. I took Pilar to the Veracruz English Library so she could borrow pronunciation tapes. We read stanzas of children's poems. I gave her short dictations. We made flashcards. I helped her fill out the temporary residence papers, went to the immigration department with her and offered to go with her to Mexico City one day to visit the Argentine consulate. But she demurred, saying she would wait to see about getting a *permiso* to immigrate to Buenos Aires until she heard from Tomás.

We found words in English so she could talk about her life, her painting technique—the small strokes she used, and her latest series called *"Fragmentos através de una Ventana"* ("Fragments through a Window") that included a painting of a red chair near a window, rain against a window, a view from a window of a ficus tree, her reflection in the window at night. Sometimes the conversations took strange turns. Their family cook making tuna *croquetas* when she was a child, watching her mother swim out to sea so far that she feared she'd never come back, her tiny apartment in the Vedado—the former maid's quarters in her childhood house before the revolution brought decay and poverty and "equality," before the house was chopped up into apartments for ten families. It was finally in these moments that I sensed she could find comfort in her past, and that my effort of listening was not only drawing her out of her resolve to not adjust, but it gave me encouragment with my task.

Summer came and went and we worked on the lessons. Sometimes she smiled, other times she was sullen. News of Argentine dissidents being killed or incarcerated trickled through the Amnesty International pipeline. I was reluctant to tell her about some of the statistics, but she always asked. She paced the living room, wringing her hands, her heavy shoes striking the linoleum floor. "I'm a prisoner still," she'd say.

I suggested she could paint or she could submit articles to art periodicals. She shook her head. Veracruz would not become a real place for her. She kept busy memorizing words and making notes of all she could remember about art in Cuba. And she checked weekly if any letters from Argentina had arrived.

After stumbling in English through the lessons, Pilar repaid me by teaching me the basics of art history. I learned how Cuban Art was a cultural blend of African, European and North American sensibilites, and that Cubism evolved out of modernism. She became another person then, she sat straighter, words flowed, her eyes glistened. When it was time for me to leave, she slumped, a melancholy expression fell across her face, she seemed to shrink back into her determination to not adjust.

In December I was transferred to Villahermosa in the south of Mexico near the Guatemalan border. Pilar's English had hardly improved—it was as if she needed to hold everything she had intact inside of her, even the new simple phrases we'd been working on. I encouraged her to visit me, but she had no interest in Mexican life, in hearing about refugees fleeing from Central America. I wrote her letters and she wrote back, but she sent only bits of her latest writing; there was never news of what she was doing to occupy herself, never much appreciation for my curiosity. The letters stopped for six months until a last one came. It was posted from Buenos Aires and was written in broken English. She decided finally to go, to take another step forward. Tomás' sister sent her a letter, and a few weeks later, an airline ticket. Tomás was still missing, but Pilar was with his family. She was joining in with their optimism that he'd just walk in the door one day. Expectation, she said, was so much better than living with despair—that enervating Cuban despair, that despair that she'd held between herself and her future, herself and me.

The Hacienda

Every night Lola escaped her mother's room and tiptoed through the *hacienda* out to the garden. She was not to be seen. She slipped silently through the dark. Everyone slept—except the man, the *patrón* of the house. The man paced in his study. Exhausted, he slumped onto a chair and stared at the wall.

At first Lola knew nothing. Her world was as wide as her mother. She remembered little of their long journey to the *hacienda*. The sun was hot. The earth was hot. The sagebrush pricked her skin. Her eyes stung from wind. She refused to walk further. Her mother hissed words, then turned away without her. Defiant, Lola watched her disappear. Puffs of dust lingered on the path. Lola struggled to her feet and followed.

A room above a kitchen. Here she had to remain, as her mother explained, to be safe from the monsters. Lola stared at the wooden crucifix on the wall, at the line of blood dripping from the man's head, his hands, his breast. She studied the cracks in the ceiling. Day followed day. She no longer felt fear. She waited.

In the evening, Lola was allowed into the kitchen, into Severiana's world. Her mother sat by herself, away from Lola, from Severiana, from the laborers. Lola dipped her tortilla in the chicken broth and listened to the conversation. It was always the same story. The death of Señora Carmen and Señor Jorge's infant son. The death that had torn the bond between the *patrón* and his wife. The Señora allowed no children around—there could be no reminder of her loss.

Severiana cooked, and laughed sometimes, her large breasts swung loosely inside her gingham blouse.

The seasons changed. Lola opened her door to the rain that clattered across the courtyard. Oh, she thought, to be the rain or to move in the air like leaves or dust. The night rain battered the roof tiles. She could not sleep through the pounding and got up, left her room and went down the back stairs into the big house. She walked past heavy carved doors, through rooms crowded with paintings, parchment lamps, chairs and couches. As she walked, she touched the velvet coverings on the furniture. Softness crushed beneath her fingers. Through the window she saw the rain had blown away. Trees bent and swayed, beckoning her.

Jorge, the *patrón*, woke from his dream. Always the dream— the diffused shadow, which he could not confront. He counted rafters and stopped when he reached the fifth. Five years. Five years in this house. His wife's house. The house in which he now felt he was a guest. The wife he was destroying. He needed to search out fresh thoughts, organize his tasks, tie himself to the *hacienda's* future. But his wife? Jorge listened for Carmen in the next room, to the silence of sorrow and separation since the death a year ago of little Jorge. This bed was no longer shared. Carmen had vanished into herself. He could not reach her, did not want to help her. Not this listless, lifeless Carmen, straightening books, tidying knickknacks, rearranging flowers in a vase, alone, beyond memory.

He thought back five years to their first meeting. He, the lost geologist driven by torrential rains, seeking shelter. Soaked, exhausted, uninvited, an apparition. The dogs barked. Carmen hurried out of her house, stood in the rain, her blouse glued to her shoulders, her skirt dripping. Her cheeks were flushed, her smile welcoming. Jorge melted into the warmth of her house. They talked into the night. Not so much of themselves, but about impressions, the geology of canyons, the Dutch landscape paintings on her wall, volcanic formations in Central Mexico. Their talk was tempered, responsive, sincere. She insisted he stay.

During the following days, they rode horses out through the rain to check on the river. They rode through cattle fields, up to a hay plateau and down through the eucalyptus alley. Jorge was transported, yet at ease. Youth and health blended into affection and soon marriage. She would no longer live alone. He would release the past and the sadness that had marked him too long. Time for energizing the *hacienda*, to bring it back to the life it had before her parents died seven years ago. Time for children.

Lola stepped from the *portal* onto the grass and felt the stringy texture under her feet. Smells of jasmine mixed with wet earth. Her heart beat fast. The sounds of crickets and the trickle of water falling from wet branches flowed. She placed leaves collected from the pond across the grass in swirling snail shell patterns and dug near a tree to store sticks and a flower petal. She heard owls and coyotes. She stood still, like a tree.

Jorge and Carmen sat at the dinner table. Severiana walked purposefully to break the silence as she served the *pozole* and tortillas. Carmen lifted her glass of port, smelled the wine, put it down. "What do you suppose the weather will be tomorrow?"

Jorge raised his eyebrows and sipped his beer. Her question about the weather was their only conversation. Carmen refolded her napkin and placed it back on her lap. She scraped a crumb from the tablecloth. Their silverware clinked against the porcelain. The clock ticked. A dog sighed in his sleep.

"I'll be gone for the day." Jorge often left to survey the cattle when he could, to escape.

Carmen sighed. Alone again, while Jorge rode in the *campo*. Though she was not sure why, his absences made her suspicious. She felt compelled to search out signs of her husband's past life, this life he refused to share, which adhered to him like wax on old furniture. She touched his books, hesitant, flipped pages in search of notes. She was certain he kept a journal, but never found it. Why did she search? For whom did she search? For a young woman he mumbled about on occasion. Natalia. A Natalia he met when he was nineteen.

Carmen dwelled on her son. She could not remember much about when he was alive. His birth was hard, but she had loved him with the clearest emotions. Now, he was always in her mind, wedged. At first, when she found him that afternoon, she could not touch him. Horrified, she and Jorge stood by the crib and looked at his still, blue face. At last she picked the boy up and clutched him to her chest. She breathed on his forehead to give him her air, her life. For hours she carried her infant, recoiling from disbelief and naked hatred before entreaties to rest, to surrender her burden. She went outside, away from the maids, away from her husband. With evening, a chill swept through the garden where she sat. She wrapped her sweater around the cold form, hugged him closer, but the body had grown stiff.

Jorge was back in the hills. The day wore on. The sweat of his horse dried, Jorge's mind slowed. His back bent with fatigue, and his thoughts returned to Carmen and the child. He understood her distance. The crazed look. Her love pouring into the dead child. Eternal affection. Affection he could no longer offer, could not share. Did his lack of love condemn the child? All affection in his possession was long given away. There was no solace. Not even in the night breeze.

He rode on, though, unaware of a gathering peace until, nearing the river, he recognized he was calm. He slid from the saddle and walked along the bank to watch the moonlight on the water.

A sound rose up to him. A sound he could not place. He strained to hear but caught only the wash of water and the light rustle of leaves. Then, by the water, he made out the figure of a young girl wearing a blue dress. Moonlight filled her face, illuminating high cheekbones and the whites of her eyes. She turned, long black hair fell about her shoulders. Intent, humming, she searched and gathered. She scooped water from the river into a small pan. She worked contentedly, sculpting the sand on the bank, extending her pebbled paths, placing here and there stems of wilted flowers.

Jorge watched the young girl. So, this was the washerwoman's child. The secret child. As he watched, something shifted in his mind. A memory became vivid. He still saw the child moving through the layers of her play, but was reminded of a second, slightly more mature girl from the past—his Natalia. Natalia in the blue dress of their first meeting, when they were eighteen, the summer their families had been invited to a lake house in Valle de Bravo.

He remembered Natalia lying on her stomach across the dock, reaching deeper and deeper, trying to fish an object from the water. Some magic in the way she reached into the water drew him to her, lured him out of his shyness and to her side. She jumped at his approach, surprised. Her hair fanned from behind her ear and blew about lightly. A hot wind pressed her dress against her thin body, her breasts. She brushed her bangs from her face. Later, there was the nutty smell in her hair and her breath on his neck, as they embraced in the boathouse at night.

Coming back to his senses, the riverbank was deserted; the girl had vanished, Natalia was gone like stone. Only water flowing down the river in the remaining night.

Carmen held her hands cupped over her face when Jorge arrived for breakfast. Severiana poured the coffee, moved the breadbasket closer to Jorge, plucked a fallen rose petal from the table, and retreated to the kitchen. Winds rustled outside. The jacaranda tree creaked. Carmen leaned back in her chair; her hand skimmed the hem of the white tablecloth as she studied Jorge. What did she admire in him? Walking with him in the fields that first year? Planning the crops and discussing where to stack the hay, the evenings he played the piano while she worked on accounting? Now she did not know; her thinking had grown thick.

"Last night I took a walk, looking for you," Carmen announced, wondering why she broke the silence. "Why do you leave?" Her voice was querulous, flat. Carmen sipped her coffee and looked out at the blossoms torn by the wind from the tree. She was aware of her dullness, the distance of her emotions.

There was a kitten in Lola's room. Lola curled around the kitten, wrapped the kitten around her neck, held the kitten in her arms. She rocked it back and forth on the rickety cot. Purring filled the room. But soon Lola grew restless and longed for the garden. She spilled the kitten onto the cot and went out. She lingered in the long hall. Smells of mildew clung to the hanging tapestries. A faint sound, a piano playing slowly and quietly tempted her into the study; she sank onto the floor. The man was there. The way the chords paused reminded her of the trees in the valley. They possessed a space between them. She remembered the alley and the thin shadows falling from the trees, growing longer as the moon rose.

"I'm playing for Natalia. Maybe you are perhaps somehow like the young Natalia, the girl she was before I knew her. I cannot forget her; my life wears away. I ruin everything around me dwelling on her memory. I cannot even remember my son."

For a moment Jorge was quiet, wondering about the need to speak to this strange child, yet feeling a freedom hearing his anxiety being spoken outloud, he continued. "I sat beside Natalia on the dock. Our shoulders touched. She hummed, dipped her toes in the water."

Jorge hesitated, aware of his voice. He looked toward Lola. She was stretched along the wall, her body partly hidden by the couch. He saw only thin brown legs. A thunderclap rumbled in the distance, rain batted the windowpanes. Lola rose to her feet and sidestepped—facing the wall so he could not see her—from the room.

Lola dressed in Carmen's discards she found in a basket in the laundry. She wore her white nightgown at night, and her sweater with buttons on cold mornings. She liked the brown high heels the best. They made her tall and old enough to be the kitten's mother. She often wrapped the kitten in a shawl and walked the length of the garage quarters in the heels and listened to the clacking sounds they made behind her.

The rain caused floods. The stables washed out. Ditches and *arroyos* roared. Jorge helped the workers build dams and move the cattle. When he came back to dinner, he was sopping wet. The electricity had failed, and now candles provided the only light. Since Carmen could not read in the dim light, she retired early. Jorge sat in the study. Later, he played the piano. The notes were slow, deliberate, just tight enough to hold a tune.

Lola strolled down the hall and watched her shadow brush against the walls in the flickering candlelight. She fixed a sash around her waist to prevent the hem from tripping her. Carmen's high heels teetered on the rough stone floor, dragging as Lola walked. She heard the piano and hesitated, but could not resist going into the room. She shuffled to a chair. He was playing the same tune as before. This time the notes resonated inside of her before he played them.

"Music is beautiful," Jorge said, continuing to play.

His was a slow, timorous voice, as if he could neither resist nor trust the return of memories. "At the lake house, Natalia and I found a homemade book of poetry; the handwritten pages were frayed, some fell to the floor. Reaching for them, I noticed a cricket beneath Natalia's chair. It was close to her foot, while her toes tapped the floor. I wanted to crush the insect; I was afraid it was an omen of bad luck. She would have laughed if she knew my concern. It was how she was. During those summers we were together, she never expressed fear."

Lola examined her leather shoes. How long will it take her feet to grow into them? Jorge played songs of childhood, tapping the keys in slow motion. Spanish matador songs, Mexican hat dance songs. The candles burned low. Lola went to sleep, breathing evenly. Her eyelids, curved like quarter moons, fluttered in early dreams. For a long time Jorge watched, breathing in unison with her. Her stick arms extended from the sleeves of Carmen's old dress like whittled branches. One shoe fell off, the other dangled on her toes. Her head was tilted onto her shoulder. Jorge spread a shawl from the couch across her before he left for his room.

"What I cannot seem to reach beyond," Jorge said to himself, to Lola, weeks later, "is that Natalia's no longer here. She's gone forever. Those times are lost." Nothing around them seemed to move. Stillness and darkness enveloped the room.

"When I heard she had died, I went to the village morgue. The attendant pulled back a sheet. I blinked, my eyes dried with disbelief. Her chest had been cut, then sewn with black cross-stitches. There was the black scar of a scorpion bite on her upper arm. Her hair was chopped off at her neck; stolen probably when she first arrived at the morgue.

"Her arms stretched out on either side, those long arms, now alabaster, now cold. I noticed her hands. Her right hand clenched into a tight fist. The fingers curled, closed. Why this death, it seemed to ask? Why now?"

Jorge hesitated. He was almost whispering.

"Seeing her drained, seeing her lifelessness, seeing how she was no more alive than the gray walls, the aluminum door, the plank that held her, I wanted to bolt, to scream, to accuse the attendant waiting in the hall. I closed my eyes. When I opened them, I saw her other hand. The left hand. The fingers curved as if cupping water. Opening. Allowing. Letting go. This hand understanding the fragility of life. This hand allowing death. Her silent wisdom. I sat at her side afraid to touch her, afraid to think, wanting to leave, afraid to leave. Yet, she was still giving, still guiding.

"When I got up to leave, I glanced at her one last time. A breeze, filtering down the stairwell, lifted the locks of bangs around her forehead. For an instant I sensed life. I imagined her breathing again, my mind tricked me into feeling hope, into thinking I'd awoken from a nightmare. But no, it was not so. And my son? Another death. Another empty soul."

Lola observed how his head was curled into his arm on the piano. The silence immobilized them, suspended them. The lamplight was dim. The night dipped into its longest moments.

Lola rose from the couch, clutched the skirt of the long dress, stepped out of her shoes and tiptoed to the piano. She looked at the tired man. Slowly, she reached out and with a finger touched Jorge on the shoulder.

A wave of warmth surged though Jorge. He settled into the feeling before he lifted his head to look at the girl. At her round quiet face. She peered right into Jorge. Her eyes grew wide and glistened.

Mirror

Carlota folded the letter she had just read, put the photograph that she couldn't bring herself to look at back into the envelope, and slipped it into the drawer. She continued to sit at her desk until the late afternoon sun came through the window of her apartment. She stood up finally, walked through the living room to her bedroom, opened the door of the armoire and stepped forward to look at herself in the mirror.

The letter was from her daughter, dated May 30th, 1997. It was the first she had heard of her since she'd given her up at birth at the Casa del Convento, in a small town north of Guadalajara. When she'd found out she was four months pregnant, she'd told lies to her father about why she felt ill in the morning and couldn't eat. She avoided him when he came home from work. She began to skip school. She ran along the river until she was breathless and bent from her side aching, thinking the fetus would break loose and leave her, but it grew and grew. Then she and her father had one of those fights about her mother, about how she had died. She blamed him for not having the means to pay for radiation treatments and insulted him for being just a poor professor. She ran away a few days later and found refuge for the rest of her pregnancy at the Casa. Seventeen years went by with Carlota hardly allowing a thought about this child.

Now, in the envelope in her drawer, was this daughter's tidy handwriting, telling her that, with her parents' permission, she had made this search for her birth mother. She had some questions she wanted to ask, she was by nature curious, she would be willing to come to Mexico City or meet her anywhere.

A Chilean banker and his wife had adopted the girl when they were living in Mexico in the '70s. Since that time, they had moved back to Santiago, where the girl went to school. They spent vacations on a farm on a lake. The girl's name was Gabriela Lorenzo, and she explained that, though she was an only child, she grew up with dogs and cats, and she liked to ride her horse in the country. She said she had just finished the *colegio* and was going to go to the University of Santiago, but before that, she had plans to travel with her senoir class to study churches and ruins in San Cristóbal de las Casas, Oaxca and Mexico City.

Gabriela was now seventeen. The same age as Carlota had been that day—after hours of contractions, after hours of assuming she was dying—the baby was born. She couldn't bring herself to look at the infant girl.

Carlota's hands shook when she read the letter, the pulse in her temple drummed. Why would this child come looking for her? What could she want? How would Carlota explain that she had left her, pushed her as much as she could out of mind. But the looping handwriting in the letter reminded her of her own handwriting style. In spite of any effort to be free of her choice, the guilt of the birth shivered through her in waves of shame. Now it occurred to her that, had it not been for her stubborn rebellion and eventual stubborn alienation toward her father, and had it not been her desperation to be adored by the boy José she had been so enamored with, these perfectly formed, polite and innocent words could not have been written.

Behind her, in the mirror, Carlota's eyes fell on the frayed back of the armchair, where she had tossed her gray sweater after work. One shoe was in the hall and the other on its side near the bathroom door. The bed was unmade, the curtain in the window half drawn. *El Mundo* magazine must have slipped onto the floor when she had fallen asleep with the light on—it was upside down, next to her basket of tattered paperback books. Now, late sun lit the hall, dust shimmered on the floor. Between the doors, two framed etchings were crooked, like boats stuck in sand at low tide. She looked into her armoire. Clothes were stuffed into and overflowing from shelves.

After the months at the Casa del Convento, Carlota decided to move to Mexico City. She found lodging in an elderly woman's house in return for doing chores and in the afternoons she frequented cafés around the University. She got in touch with her father and informed him of her desire to make her life in the city, to get a degree at the University, and he, relieved that she had direction, sent her an allowance once a month. She hid her thin, hungry self under knee-length sweaters and jeans, told her few acquaintances that she was a student, and soon found part-time work in a secondhand bookstore. Loneliness seeped into her. To stave it off, she devoured books, lived vicariously inside characters' lives, memorized plots. She daydreamed of country houses and of big families. Ideas began to intrigue her. What was existentialism? What did it mean that human beings create meaning in their own lives? What was a true self or a false self? Which of those selves was harboring her secret? Did the illegitimate childbirth define her, limit her, confine her? In those days, before the student uprising, she was not alone in her discretion; keeping quiet had become the way. People hid their political opinions, held secret meetings to discuss writers or freedom to print controversial stories. No one would know that she had given birth, that she had left a child to an unknown fate. She would not let it have relevance in her life.

She often dreamed of holding something warm, or being held, but the sensation dissolved. The image slivered through her sleep. When she woke, she was cold, empty; solitude gnawed at her. One night, when it was raining and she thought she had lost the key to her first real apartment, she sat in the foyer of the building and was overcome with thoughts and regrets about her father. A few days later, she took the train north for a weekend in Guadalajara.

Her father had just returned after a six-month sabbatical in Colombia. The apartment had been shut while he was gone, newspapers were piled by the kitchen door, his desk was overflowing with open books. He was exhausted, contemplating retirement from his position at the University, feeling outraged at the government, and lighting one cigarette after another. Other than the fights they'd had when she was a teenager, she did not remember seeing him so tight, so nervous.

The first afternoon she was in Guadalajara, Carlota suggested they walk to the river. She asked about her mother, what it was like when they were students, but her father shook his head.

"It does not matter anymore," he said. He walked on, as if he did not notice she was with him. And when she said that it did matter, that details make up the past, he didn't answer right away.

"But you left," he said. "You wanted to make your own way, an indication that it did not matter."

And there it was. Her mother, so few memories. Her father,

a man who did not have a chance to be the father he might have been. Herself, a flawed daughter. They stood by the river and watched the current. All thoughts, all questions, all memories entangled inside her.

"Images vanish," she said. "Tell me about Mamá. How you met. Tell me about how she used to read to me. What it was like after dinner when she listened to your philosophical theories. What was your childhood like in Colombia? Remind me how you walked me back and forth on the balcony when I couldn't sleep. And how when Mamá was sick, you dressed her, fed her, carried her to the living room while both of you pretended all was fine. How did you have that courage?" Carlota paused for a moment. Her pulse was rushing.

"I was ten," she said. "That's so long ago."

Her father turned from her and crossed his arms. He began to walk away, appeared to think better of it and turned back. "I can't do this, Carlota. I've learned not to reminisce. Those times are gone. I don't want to remember."

Carlota planned to return on Sunday to Mexico City. When she announced which train she was going to take, her father collapsed onto the couch and sighed. It then became clear to Carlota that even now there was not room for her in her childhood home.

"I had to leave," she said, to explain that day when she had disappeared.

Her father scratched his forehead. "I know," he said. "The administration from the Casa contacted me. I didn't know how to handle you. I couldn't control my confusion about bringing you up alone, and so, sadly, I didn't do anything right. But I went to visit you and then lost my nerve. I watched you in the convent garden, watched you fill the bird feeders, watched as you walked back to the chapel and disappeared through the dark vestibule." He paused as if to catch his breath.

"It was not easy, I know. I admire your honesty. You are like your mother."

Carlota, content to be back in her own space, unwrapped the mementos she'd brought from her father's apartment: a quilt, a vase, photographs of her parents and herself when they were a family. She hung two etchings of her mother's profile her father had given her, spread the quilt on her bed and arranged a bunch of yellow roses in the vase.

What became constant in those years was her bookstore job. It allowed her to study for the two classes she had begun to take. The store was not far from her apartment; she could walk home alone through the streets. Often, she'd only see a cat or two or other people who worked late. The air was fresh after the closed atmosphere in the office.

She had gone on dates, had five or so good friends, but never imagined what feeling comfortable with someone could be like until Julio came up to her after work one night. He'd reminded her that he had spoken to her earlier, in the bookstore. He was from Paraguay and worked as a project architect in a hotel development. It was his vacation; he had six weeks, he had decided to come to Mexico.

"You're lovely," Julio said to her the first morning after he stayed with her. She smiled; her mother used to tell her that. She remembered, too, when she was young, her father telling her that she was "as pretty as can be."

She dressed as Julio made coffee, toasted bread, found butter and jam. He set the table with her chipped plates and mismatched cups. "My hobby is cooking," he announced, as he pulled the chair out for her to sit down. In the following days, they discovered markets she'd never seen. He shopped for spicy tamales and stringy Oaxacan cheese. He bought her gifts—a clay casserole, kitchen towels—and at an antique fair he bought a jigsaw puzzle of a seascape.

"Puzzles are good for the brain," he announced as he arranged the pieces on her desk. They worked on the landscape, filling in the sky and then waves and palm trees.

Some evenings they walked in the streets in the Colonia San Angel or ate in sidewalk restaurants in Polanco. One weekend they spent a night in a *hacienda* near Puebla before they hiked up to the base of the volcano, Popocatepetl. Twice they visited the Anthropology Museum, and on Carlota's days off they took a bus to Toluca to see the silver shops, walked in Chapultepec Park, or visited artists' studios in Colonia Chimalistac.

One night she came home from work to find Julio sitting on the couch reading one of her favorite books, *The Labryinth of Solitude*, by Octavio Paz. She sat down beside him, leaned into his shoulder and kissed him. And then, when he left to return to his work, to his life, the air, the ease, the spontaneity was gone from her apartment. She didn't move anything; the wooden seascape with its five missing pieces remained on the desk, dish towels were where Julio last folded them, the casserole sat unwashed until she decided he would not approve of her sloppiness.

Time stopped. He would not come back. His life had moved on in the direction it had always been heading—a career and family in his own country. The sadness Carlota fell into was familiar, like the weight of life after her mother. His departure was inevitable, but she had hoped it would never happen. For a while, Carlota stayed as much as she could in her apartment, ate only apples and bread, flipped pages of books, paced, stared out the window, got up late. But one morning while drinking coffee, she made a list: an English literature class she'd take, concerts she could attend, she'd invite friends for dinner and use the cookbook Julio had given her.

She attended school full time, graduated from the University Autónoma and became a junior editor in a publishing house. A few years later she got a second degree in Spanish literature by taking courses in the evenings. Weekends were spent studying or having dinner with friends. In the spring she made a ritual of taking the train with her friends to the beach in Ixtapa. She stopped talking to Julio in her mind and found she could see textures and forms and have ideas for herself.

But now—years later, with a promotion and a routine she'd grown used to—standing in front of her mess of unfolded clothes in the armoire, Carlota felt caught. No one knew her secret. She turned around and saw the disheveled state of what was still just a student apartment. She grabbed the sweater and folded it. She picked up her shoes, pulled back the curtains, cracked the windows, organized the kitchen.

Then, she did what she had put off doing all afternoon and evening.

She opened the drawer, picked up the envelope, spread the letter on the desk and took out the photograph of Gabriela. At first glance, she saw the form of a girl dressed for riding next to a horse in front of an alley of poplar trees. It was evening when the photo had been taken; warm light lit the face, the blue eyes, dimple and dark curls. Her smile radiated from the emulsion of the image as if she were in the room. Carlota recognized it was not just the girl she saw, it was herself in a mirror.

Pablo's Feet

"Yes, Señora, I pray for someone at church," said Lupe.

Valerie had come up to the maid's terrace to ask Lupe to stop at the market after she attended Mass, and instead she was asking questions. Lupe had been pinching dead leaves from her scraggly plants lined up in coffee cans on the brick wall. "This evening I will pray for my brother Pablo. His feet have infection; he has sores. On weekends I wash the feet. The *curandera* gave me salts." Lupe filled her left hand with the crackly geranium leaves until bits began to fall.

Valerie—who had not been brought up with religion other than going to church for weddings and funerals—never really thought about Catholicism. She was surprised she'd become curious about beliefs. She wanted to know why Lupe prayed. She wanted to know if the lingering smell of dying lilies in the little church at the bottom of their cobblestone street consoled her. She wondered if Lupe knelt in front of the homemade altar of candles and a cross in her room. But Valerie was a twenty-eight-year-old American who had moved to Mexico from the Midwest. She did not yet speak Spanish. Andrew, her husband, traveled daily to Toluca, Puebla or Queretero, selling packaging materials to cereal factories. She was left in the house to be the Señora.

During the first months, she was restless and could not accept that Lupe was on her hands and knees washing the floor with a brush, or that Lupe was rubbing their clothes on the tin washboard in the sink in the garage. To escape her guilt, Valerie walked around San Angel—the colonial neighborhood—where they lived.

Enchanted by the meandering streets and pastel-colored walls, she took photographs of arched windows, and drew sketches of balconies and doors on a pad she kept in her bag. Twice a week she carried straw bags from the market full of chilies, zucchini, tomatoes and chunks of meat that the butcher had slashed off one of the beef carcasses hanging from a hook. On many afternoons she sat in the park in front of the church and listened for the five o'clock bells that rang and rang, announcing the afternoon Mass. Near the entrance, an Indian woman— wearing a brown cotton poncho—flipped fat pancakes on a portable grill, and little girls ran around the flower beds of the church courtyard playing tag, their braids flying in the air; a balloon vendor wove his way through the benches, sometimes stopping to sell his twisted dachshund or monkey-shaped balloons.

Valerie found a café where she liked to go to read. She watched a group of young women. Elegant, in high heels and matching purses, they smoked, tapping their ashes with red enameled fingernails, their dark hair pulled back into matador buns. Words flew from their mouths—the sounds curled and rolled and exclaimed, their Spanish undulated in lyrical singsong verses. Valerie listened and then returned to her book.

In June it began to rain. On one of Valerie's excursions around San Angel, she bought the famous book, *The Conquest of*

New Spain, by Bernal Diaz del Castillo. It sat on the table for a few weeks until one day she came back from a walk, soaked and chilled, to find that Lupe had lit a fire in the study. She picked up the book and began to learn about the Spaniard, Hernánd Cortés, and the conquest of Mexico.

An hour or so later, Lupe padded across the room.

"Señora," she said, "I thought you might like tea."

It was what Valerie craved, though she never would have wanted to bother Lupe with a request. She was touched. Lupe placed the tray on the table and took the top off of the sugar bowl.

"*Hay leche, sí usted quiere.*" She went back to the kitchen to get the pitcher of milk. It was then, at that moment, that Valerie looked at her closely.

She was, of course, the "maid," the person whose presence had changed Valerie's status. Valerie had never even thought of having a maid, but all day long peddlers selling everything from hot potatoes to handmade pottery rang the bell. All day she could hear the whistle of the knife sharpener, the call of the man selling tortillas, or the chant of a tin pot salesman. They roamed the streets, they had their routes, they rang doorbells. Someone had to be there, or the house would be deemed empty; a robbery might occur. Now Valerie no longer made the bed, washed the dishes or cooked. She didn't even open the front door. She could not get a job without a visa, had no great talents, and other than Spanish lessons at the Instituto Americano, her time was her own.

When Andrew came home late in the evening he filled her with his stories—traffic jams on the road to Toluca, fresh snow on the crest of the volcano. He'd come through the door, handsome in his suit, energized by how fluent his Spanish was becoming, ready for a quiet evening. They laughed at themselves. They felt like grown-ups, sipping tequila and *limon* on the terrace, talking about impressions of Mexico, before moving to the dining room and being served a tortilla pie or *arroz con pollo* that Lupe had cooked.

As Lupe handed Valerie the cup of tea, Valerie noticed her slender hands, the perfectly trimmed pearl-shaped nails. She was wearing an embroidered blouse and a blue-and-white-checkered apron over her skirt. Lupe poured milk into Valerie's tea, placed the pitcher on the tray and turned to tend the fire. Her long, thick braid fell forward and caught for a moment on the ruffle of her sleeve. Logs in the fireplace—stacked like a pyramid— collapsed. Lupe added two twisted mesquite branches, stirred the embers and waited for the wood to catch fire before returning the poker to its place.

"Con permiso"—with your permission—she said bowing her head, as she left for the kitchen.

The room felt suddenly lonely. It was a room in which Valerie had always been alone; it was where her desk was, where she wrote verb declensions, read in the afternoon and stacked her books. Rain battered the windows. From the couch, she saw jacaranda branches in the garden bending in the wind. Lupe had turned on the lamps before she got home; soft light spread to the creamy plaster arch of the ceiling and onto the little colonial chest—their first antique—bought in Puebla. *The Conquest of New Spain* was on her lap. She flipped past the arrival of Cortez's ship and found the page where the Spanish entourage walked into Montezuma's palace in what is now Mexico City. The awe of the European horses and the Aztec ruler's anticipation of the arrival of a new god dazzled and blinded Montezuma. He opened his arms to Cortez, and with that gesture the Aztec Empire was never the same. Christianity had arrived.

Late in the day the rain stopped. Valerie walked down the slippery cobblestones to the church. Mass was over and people were streaming out into the park. A sea of colorful *rebozos*—hand-woven wool shawls worn by the Indian ladies emerging through the wooden church doors—brightened up the gray evening. Valerie watched the people scatter; a few went down to Avenida Revolucion, some walked off in the direction of the *mercado*. She looked for the women from the café, but they were not there. A lone woman, whose head was covered in a red shawl, started up Calle Galeana in the direction of their house. It was Lupe.

Valerie picked up her pace to catch up but became shy. What would she say in her broken Spanish? She had few words. She watched Lupe make her way over the cobblestones and then decided to hurry.

"Lupe!" she said, "*Soy yo.*" She stopped. Lupe smiled, revealing a crooked front tooth.

"You were at church?"

"*Sí. La iglesia.*"

Together, silently, they returned to the house.

There, Valerie collected her phrase book, returned to the kitchen and sat down on a stool. They began to talk. The function of a sink, the contents of a refrigerator, the use of a hand mixer, the brown glaze on the *cazuela*. Valerie copied Lupe's pronunciation, repeating the words. Meanwhile, Lupe stirred beans cooking in a clay pot. She sorted through dried herbs on the windowsill. "*Epazote,*" she said, "It grows along the roads in our *ranchito*." Valerie smelled it. The odor was faint, like a weed. Lupe broke up the branch and put it in with the beans. She pulverized red chilies with a mortar and pestle, put chicken breasts into another pot, added water, chilies, chopped onions, charred tomatoes and then lit a match to light the back burner.

"*Molcajete*," she said pointing to the chiseled volcanic–stone bowl she used for making salsa. Bit by bit, during the afternoons for the next year, the terms and names—a few Nàhuatl ones, the ancient Aztec language of Central Mexico—but mostly Spanish—began to make enough sense that Valerie could string them together into sentences. She could have a conversation about Lupe's life.

"I pray that Pablo's feet will work again. He cannot walk. The pain is like knives," Lupe said in her whispering voice as she trimmed leaves from the next plant. Valerie learned that he was her oldest brother; the two other brothers had moved away. Pablo lived with their mother in the family *ranchito*. Lupe pulled out from her apron pocket a wrinkled, faded photograph of her mother when she was in her forties, she said. Her mother was standing in front of a house not much larger than the maid's room where Lupe stayed. They looked at the photo for a few moments before the sun set on the maid's terrace, leaving them in the cool of a shadow. Lupe moved two of the coffee can flower pots from the balcony wall and placed them under the overhang.

"Where do you stay when you go there? There's not room for more than two people."

Lupe looked at Valerie and furrowed her brow.

"Yes. It is a small *ranchito*. *Muy pequeño*."

Suddenly, Valerie said, " I'd like to see where you live. Can you take me sometime?"

"Oh no, Señora, " Lupe stammered, as she turned to adjust another can. "It would not be *bueno*. It is not a place for a Señora."

"Maybe then a trip to your village?" Valerie said. She felt a rush of excitement; she would see rural Mexico.

"It is a very small village. My mother is busy with Pablo. It is too hot there." Lupe added.

They had to travel on four buses to arrive at the stop nearest Lupe's house. Valerie had no idea where they were going, she didn't care; it had taken her another six months from her first request to convince Lupe to let her go home with her. During those months, Lupe became more talkative. Lupe's sentences were short. She'd be heating up a taco, when she suddenly offered that her father had left them. He'd worked in a tortilla factory. Went to work one day, and never came back. Or when she was pinning clothes on the line one day while Valerie was in the laundry yard, Lupe told how her mother washes clothes in the stream. It had been her job as a child to spread sheets on bushes to dry. Valerie learned that the nights in winter are cold, a wind blows across their plateau. She pictured the children sleeping near each other under rough wool blankets. Valerie told Lupe about the little farms tucked in the hills of Kentucky and that the farmers had cows and chickens and goats. When she tried to describe how church services sometimes took place in tents that traveled from town to town and how the congregation sang the hymns, she could see that Lupe could not imagine life beyond what she had experienced. Lupe shook her head and said, "A Mass is in an *iglesia*. God made the churches."

The first bus headed west out of Mexico City in the direction of Toluca. The second bus went south. The third route twisted over a parched plateau. The buses were jammed. Scratchy music played on the radio. Chickens stuffed into baskets, women holding babies with dirty diapers, and men reeking of alcohol shared the seats or stood in the aisle. They got off at a crumbling shell-shaped plaster shrine. Lupe crossed herself, muttered a prayer and adjusted the faded plastic flowers in the niche.

On the bus, Lupe retold Valerie the story of how she'd left home when she was fourteen to work. Every Sunday—her day off—she brought home her pesos. Half of their house burned twenty years ago; Pablo was at fault; he used to drink; he had done something bad. Now he couldn't even walk to get mescal. Lupe grinned as she spoke, as if the memories were so far away that they did not belong to her anymore.

They walked up a rutted road. Two men leading donkeys loaded with scraps of wood passed. In the distance Valerie saw a hamlet, a collection of shacks along a dry *arroyo*.

"The *ranchito*," Lupe pointed. A burro brayed. Dust rose up around their ankles. An emaciated dog stood up and teetered after them. Valerie looked beyond the cluster of houses and saw dry, low hills along the horizon. Children ran down the street as soon as they noticed that an *estranjera* was walking their way.

"*Es americana,*" Lupe told them. They laughed, covering their rotten teeth with their hands. One of them picked up a stone and threw it at the dog.

Valerie recognized the patched-earth house of Lupe's photograph. A barefoot boy held the waist of his torn pants as he ran ahead to alert the neighbors of their arrival. Lupe's mother came out the door and stood like a statue under the tin roof. Lupe addressed her in a few words of Nàhuatl, but her mother did not react or move.

"*Buenos días,*" Valerie said. Lupe's mother's hands hung by her side, she stood squarely over her huarache sandals, her muslin skirt was stained with years of use. She wore an embroidered blouse, her face was angular like Lupe's, but her braid was at least twelve inches longer; it fell to her knee. She would not look at Valerie. She did not take her hand.

"*Está en su casa,*" she said turning away. She went through the door.

They stepped from a brilliant blue Mexican day into the dark house. A sour smell filled the room. Valerie recalled Pablo's infected feet. She saw a crumpled man, Pablo, hunched in the corner on a cot. When her eyes became accustomed to the shadowy light, she looked around. Other than the bed, the only furniture was a pile of bedding, a table, two chairs, a stool and a two-burner stove. A tattered calendar with a picture of the Virgin of Guadalupe hung by the single window.

Now Valerie understood Lupe's reticence about her visit. She had come to a place she did not belong and was not welcome. She had expected to be charmed by village life, but the dankness, the squalor and the smell of the room made her dizzy. She looked at Pablo and saw his feet. They were swollen, blackened and round like bruised melons.

"*Buenos días,*" he mumbled, but Valerie couldn't respond. She couldn't help but look at his feet.

The sound of a chair scraping the dirt floor and then Lupe's offer that she sit allowed her to turn and look out the door. A hot breeze stirred the air. She could breathe normally again. The brother, her mother, and the crude furnishings seemed flat—

caught—in sepia tones. No color seeped in. Except for Lupe. Here especially, her stoic Indian beauty, her straight nose and almond skin radiated. Her dark eyes sparkled. Her smile and careful words filled the awkwardness. She did not seem to notice how tongue-tied Valerie had become. She did not seem to care that her mother was stiff and removed and stood in the corner stirring the pot of food, looking straight ahead at the chipped brick behind the stove. Lupe chatted to Pablo, slipping between Nàhuatl and Spanish, filling him with details he could savor until she returned the next Sunday. He responded with grunts, but when Valerie dared to look at him, she saw a faint smile on his face.

Valerie ate by herself at the table, and Lupe, as usual, served her. Each bite dried in her throat. The meat with the chocolate-colored chili sauce was hard to chew, but the tortillas that her mother had rounded into balls, flattened in a hand press and heated up over the flame were puffed and slightly charred; they melted into the sauce.

After lunch, Lupe left to go to the village water faucet. Valerie walked outside and offered to help, but Lupe refused. Valerie stood in the sun, on the bare patch of yard. She felt faint, weak. Soon, Lupe lumbered her way up to the house with water sloshing in buckets. Valerie followed her inside.

Lupe pulled a large pan from under the bed, dumped the water and a handful of healing salts into it. She lifted first one and then the other of Pablo's feet into the pan. A high-pitched cry pierced the air. The salts cut into his sores. He clenched the blanket on the bed, his eyes rolled to the side. He moaned.

Valerie stood by the table, not knowing what to do. Should she avert her glance? Was it wrong to look? Lupe cupped Pablo's foot in her left hand, and with her right hand dipped a rag into the water, raised it up, and squeezed it. Pablo burst out crying, but perhaps remembering there was a guest, he held his hand over his mouth, while Lupe made calming, hushing sounds. Valerie watched Lupe's long, slender fingers with her pearl-shaped nails massage her brother's ankles. She watched her wrap the feet into two towels and place them gently onto the floor. She watched how she held each wrapped foot for a few moments. She watched Lupe bow her head.

"There," she said to Pablo, "It is good I am here today so I can wash your feet. I pray to God to make them better. I pray to God to help you walk."

Lupe stood up, carried the pan out to the porch and threw the water into the yard.

Valerie was alone with Pablo. She wanted to say something, to fill the void, but words would not have come even if she had tried. Her eyes stung, her temples pounded. The rotten odor pervaded the room. This pain, she wondered. This agony. Agony medicine could alleviate. This man dependent like a child. The water tossed into dirt.

Valerie left the *casita*, went to the edge of the yard. She looked at the *arroyo* below her. Regaining focus, she took a deep breath, returned to the house and said to Lupe, "I can help. Pablo can go to a clinic. I'm sure he'll walk again."

Lupe looked down, she crossed herself, a half-smile flickered on her face. Perhaps not hearing, perhaps not wanting to hear, she said, "It would be a miracle if he could walk; it would be a blessing; it would be *gracias a Dios*."

Our Father

When we arrived the rain stopped, the harbor was eerily calm; palm fronds and grasses along the shore were bent. Sun seeped through the mist and stung our eyes, blinding us in the tropical glaze. A shout of a voice I recognized but had not heard for years called our names; Magalena, Soledad, Nina, and then my mother's name, Dominga, rang in my ears. Only my mother and Soledad could see over the railing. The rest of us were too young or too short; the revolution had kept us lean.

Other passengers on deck began to shout, waving in hopes of finding those they knew. Small wooden boats were rowed alongside; naked-chested men held up fish for sale. The cargo hold was opened; there were shouts and orders of what to unload. Sugar cane was lowered onto transport scows; bales of tobacco passed from man to man to the dock. A wooden crate of citrus fruit fell on the rail and broke apart. Grapefruit bobbed in the water.

Mother held Magalena at the rail. Soledad, the eldest of us three girls, hung back with Pedro, the eleven-month-old baby. We could see the docks, the Mayan longshoremen pushing carts, spraying water on hulls of ships, coiling ropes. My mother pointed out the people on shore waiting for the boat. She dabbed her eyes and waved her arms. We tugged her sleeve to let us see more, to look for *him*. I had never before seen excitement coming from her.

I saw our father before the others did. He was standing in front, his hands shielding his eyes from the glare. I wondered if there was anything about me he recognized, if he could feel my reticence. He had disappeared before we were moved to the countryside, before my mother was sick. Soledad worked in the cane fields, so I stayed by my mother, wiped her brow, covered her as she shook, fanned her when she sweated. This moment in the harbor did not mean the same for me as it did for Soledad, to whom my father had read stories when she was young, or for Magalena who was only two when he left.

We had endured the humiliations of the revolution's relentless vision, were made only weaker, more cowed, and more terrified by threats of prison camps, stories of friends imprisoned who'd not gotten out. Yet nothing would ever scare me more than seeing my mother come apart after our father disappeared. Her screams, clumps of hair in her hands, food not touched, walls punctured where she kicked. I did not grow mature from caring for her, feeding her and helping her with Magalena.

In time she gathered strength. I withdrew. I disobeyed, hid under the house, ran off from my job in the fields. To pay, I carried buckets of night soil from latrines, the slosh spilling on my feet, stinging cuts. At meals I sat alone, away from others, in the silence of my own body. When neighbors claimed I'd get over living without a father, I did not respond.

Soledad spotted my father and handed the baby back to me and began to jump and wave her arms too. She knew how our father adored her—his first child. I only remembered his impatience and frustration and annoyance with the revolution. How he swore, how he paced, how he wrote and wrote at night at the table. Magalena did not yet talk when he had left. Now, she begged to be lifted to see over the rail and cried, *"Dónde, dónde está Papá?"* Pedro—placed on the deck between us—began to cry. The noise, the sudden screaming, the horns and cries coming from the harbor, were confusing. The boat that had pitched for the last days in storms and waves was now stationary. Pedro was no longer strapped into a berth.

Six years had passed since that day we last saw our father. He had been in touch only recently, planning how to get us out of Cuba. The letters were written in code and took months for informers to get them to the sugar cane factory. My mother never could complain, never could tell him about the days she writhed, her wild hair, her unfocused eyes, the hostel we shared with other families, whooping cough, hunger, black nights, the soldiers, her night duty, Pedro.

I was glad there were now a few moments left of our little family before my father would learn about Pedro. Since I did not know Papá anymore and my mother would not talk about him, I wasn't sure what would happen. It was frightening to think how he would take over our lives; like the soldier, keeping my mother down, those grunts, the sighs, her tears. Our father might care most about Soledad, teach her again about history; he'd be charmed by eight-year-old Magalena, who was the same age now as Soledad when he left.

He must have been feeling relief; his plan worked, we had arrived. No extra clothes, no comb, no shoes for Pedro. Yet we were there, he could see us on deck waving, my mother lifting Magalena, and Soledad calling out to him, our heads bobbing up and down. But his life alone was still intact. A part of me wanted to pick up Pedro and hold him high enough for my father to see, to warn him. I'd seen men after their wives got pregnant by those soldiers. I'd seen those wives beaten.

A launch from the Immigration Bureau came out to the boat. We were to spend the night on board; La Facilidad de Inmigración did not have room for us. The fishing boats were sent away, a quarantine flag was raised, an anchor dropped into the bay. That night was further reminder of our endless passage, our lives in the '60s. We were corralled back into the hold, into the smell of vomit scrubbed with disinfectant and the starchy odor of over cooked rice. Pedro would not stay in our laps, he had to be strapped into the berth. He screamed. Other boat people, who before had been too scared to complain, hissed at us. No one slept in that furnace of sweating bodies. The glassy harbor made every cough, snore and use of the over flowing bucket audible.

I had a dream about my father. He was on the boat with us during the passage but was tied to a mast. A storm tossed us back and forth; we were thrown in the hold from side to side, turned blue with bruises, cried for help, but he could not move, did not try. When I woke, my head was heavy, my heart beating, my shirt sopped.

At noon the next day, when the humidity had settled and a thick wind blew, the launch came back. Uniformed men prodded us like cattle onto the sweltering planks of their boat. The harbor was churning with waves brewing before the next downpour. Those who had recovered from seasickness were again pale. Starving, weak from the voyage, cast between an era of intimidation and now this unknown country—that might only admit us after we had lost all hope—we looked with trepidation to what might come.

We were exhausted, and like most exhausted people we knew we had little energy to sustain the jabs and questioning and indifference of bureaucrats. We arrived at La Facilidad and were herded into a steel shed. It was as heartless as the third class hold of the cargo boat. Long narrow windows near the ceiling offered little light. Six folding tables, where we were to line up for examination, separated the room in two. Examiners asked us questions, poked our abdomens, made us cough, gagged our throats and examined the women behind flimsy screens. Men with broken fingernails scratched our hair for lice.

My mother was taken aside and asked questions about her children, her husband, her affiliations with the communists. Clerks, in loose, sweat-stained suits, sat in a room with a partition. My mother was on one side. My father—whom we had not seen but from a distance the day before on the dock—on the other side. Their answers compared.

Suddenly everything came to a stop. One of the clerks stood up and walked off, shaking his head. Another kept looking at his notes. My mother fidgeted, looked at us lined up on a metal bench along the wall of the cubicle. Her face was flushed, confused. She jerked when spoken to, she bit her index finger, she shook her hand, she bit her finger again. The clerk lowered his glare, his accusing expression. He was following rules, he said, she was complicating them. He wiped perspiration from his brow with a handkerchief and blew his nose. Then he stated the problem.

"Your husband has requested immigration for three children. You have four. How can that be?"

My mother started to cry. She covered her mouth, to hide lost teeth, to hide fear. But fear shot through her eyes. In a stuttering voice, she mumbled about the Cuban solider. Her night duty. The clerk stared at my mother. He furrowed his brow, tilted his wobbly chair back while flicking the edge of the file with his thumb.

We waited, not knowing what was happening on the other side. The clerk got up, went to my father's side, came back and compared notes with another clerk. A thin, sly smile crept across his lips. "You may go. Your husband says four." My mother picked up Pedro; we followed her through the narrow door to meet our father.

All the waving and excitement of yesterday pressed back into us. My father knelt down and opened his arms to us girls. We went to him. I felt love I had not remembered. He looked exhausted, had tears in his eyes. He hugged us until it hurt. But when he stood up he seemed old, stricken. He did not look at mother, did not greet her.

He knelt down a second time and pulled us to him, and then one by one looked at us and one by one put his right hand on our heads. Mother, holding Pedro, stood behind him, her face frozen. I wanted to go to her but could not resist him. He pulled bright blue neck scarves from his pocket and tied them around our necks; the fourth scarf—the one for my mother—he stuffed back in his pocket. He turned and glanced at her. His mouth curled down, words gurgled in his throat but did not come out. His eyes fell.

He began to walk, and we marched behind him to the ferry dock. We took one bus from the terminal to another outside the city. There we changed to a bigger bus that wound through streets crowded with women begging, with children selling chewing gum. From a square we walked past stores and stands where people held out pineapples and coconuts for sale. We walked and walked, the streets got narrower, laundry hung between buildings. The scarves made us stand out. We wanted to take them off, it was hot. I unknotted mine, our father saw me, shook his head. We continued single file past merchants and shoppers, women in woven blouses and heavy rubber-soled sandals, men in wide straw hats. We went past stalls of chilies and dried fruits, past Indians selling chickens in wire cages.

We walked up five floors in a dirty cement stairway and came to a back door and entered into what smelled like the house of a stranger. The windows were cracked; a ceiling fan stirred stale air. We stood by the wall, not knowing where to look, where to go. My mother, holding Pedro, stayed by the door. The furniture was scraped bare of paint, tattered books were stacked on the floor, a typewriter was on a low table.

Looking at us standing there, my father began to cry. He cried into the crook of his arm, turning his back so we couldn't see.

Then he emptied his pockets of his change, put the blue scarf and keys onto the table and lit the gas burner. Steam puffed from the pot. He served us tortillas and beans and melon. We shoveled the food into our mouths, tasting flavors we'd rarely had, with a hunger only starving people know and weak with the suspicion that it was a dream and that we'd wake up and have only our allotment of rice again.

He gave us new clothes, shoes that were too small, pants and cotton ponchos, but he did not unfold the blouse for my mother. He put it aside. The light drained from the room, stillness overcame us. We sat and waited, for what we did not know. We had no expectations. Sadness hung on the grimy walls, the sagging chairs. It started to rain hard.

Pedro wiggled from my mother's grip and crawled across the room. He began to chatter the way he used to before we left. The fatigue in our bones, to the pounding of the rain paralyzed us. Pedro sensed we were all looking at him, but not gleaning anguish; he beamed. He crawled to the table, grabbed the scarf, sat down and whirled it, his eyes following the movement of the blue fluttering. He held it around his collar and looked at Magalena and Soledad and me—as if imploring us to help him fasten it—but it was our father who sat down on the floor near him and tied the scarf around Pedro's neck.

A Day

His job was to rise at five in the morning to sweep the cobble-stones in front of the house. Then he threw buckets of water onto the tiled terraces, wiped the iron garden chairs with a cloth, cleaned dust from the windows, trimmed grass with scissors, pulled dead leaves from the bougainvillea vines, cleaned ashes from the fireplaces, brought wood from the cellar, laid the fires. He mopped the dining room and living room floors, he waxed the wooden stairs, and when the dog came down from his master and mistress's bed, he let it into the garden and then picked up after it. He followed the cook to the market, carrying home baskets of coconuts and papaya and meat shanks. Back from the market, he swept the servants' patio, carried buckets of hot water from the kitchen stove down to the laundry. He collected the garbage in a tall basket, lifted it to his shoulder and steadied the burden by looping a band across his forehead. He walked for a half an hour to the edge of the town, to one of those side roads too rutted for cars, to dump the load. Midday, he took the dog on a walk around the *barrio*. He bathed the dog in the garage, dried the dog with the *patróna's* towels, fed the dog before letting it back into the house. He vacuumed the *patróna's* car, hosed it clean, waxed it, rubbed it with a chamois cloth. If the wind blew, he raked the garden, filled the basket with leaves, hiked the bas-ket up to his shoulders, adjusted the band, walked out of the city to the rutted road. Evenings, he lit the fires, dusted the lanterns, mopped the kitchen, cleaned the pots and pans, cloroxed the servants' lavatory, shined the brass door knocker, stacked wood, split kindling. He ate leftover tortillas and *pozole* from a bowl the cook left for him in the servants' patio. When all was quiet, when the lights of the house went dark, when the dog had been one last time in the garden, he crawled under a shelf by the entry, curled into a poncho and slept the sleep of a man who, during the day, never rested, never said a word, never was noticed, did not dream.

Wherever

Eugenia lived in her own realm. There she always was when we went out to the finca to visit her and our grandmother. Eugenia was large and quiet, with her knotted hair calmed under a hairnet and wearing a Mayan shawl instead of a blouse over her flattened breasts. When spoken to her gaze roamed the room, landing first, it seemed, on the windows that framed the courtyard, before floating over the faces of whoever had come to visit. Her simple response of "*sí*" or "*no*" spilled from her mouth in a long flow; the words slurred into a deep hum that rippled the creamy skin on her chest. She spent most of her days sitting in a wicker chair in the *sala*, sewing intricate stitches into linen blouses she never wore.

In the afternoons, she took the stitches out one by one, maneuvering the needle skillfully with her chubby fingers. Occasionally, she rose from the chair and in slow motion made her way across the creaking wooden floor to the piano. She shuffled the sheets of music until she found what she wanted and then played with an ease the rest of her life lacked—an ease that had drained from her when she had moved back to Mexico City after five years of living in Rio de Janeiro. There, we were told, she had not only spoken Portuguese, but in her music classes she had learned German. Now, the only time she picked up a pencil was to write a date on either the Brahms Concerto No. 1 or the Mozart Piano Concerto in D Minor that she had just played.

The date though was from her Brazilian days and was written in German or Portuguese.

In the evening, when the sun sank beneath the garden wall, the maid brought them a sherry. When we were there at that hour, we heard our grandmother tell Eugenia about life beyond their house. She chatted about Eugenia's two brothers (our fathers), their experiences in universities in the States, the women they married in the late forties and finally all about us, the children they had in the fifties. Our grandmother always named our names, but Eugenia didn't appear to know who was who. Sometimes she clutched her leather album of her days at the music conservatory in Rio. Sometimes she tapped her fingers on the arm of the chair. She stared at the sepia photographs she had taken of the beach, cafés on narrow streets and exotic plants in the botanical gardens. Her postcard-size sketchbook of drawings of hats—evidently she loved hats—was kept in her sewing basket. If we asked to look at it, she didn't seem to care to hear and looked beyond us, as if she were watching a life that was taking place elsewhere.

We never knew what triggered her withdrawal from reality, other than that it had happened at a time when our grandmother requested she return to settle down and perhaps get married. She did come home dutifully, but her mind started to slide. One morning she woke up screaming. Later, she fell into day-long and then week-long silences. We were told that she spent those first days sitting on a ladder-back chair in her room with the curtains drawn, staring at the wall. Our fathers told us how she claimed she heard bugs in the walls scratching messages she could not translate. In the summer of 1946, our grandmother took her to Switzerland, to a clinic for the summer where she was given shock treatments that assuaged her fears but also depleted her energy.

We wondered if she had had a handsome opera singer fiancé in Rio. From photographs we could see she had been beautiful, her prominent cheekbones rosy, her skin almond. Thick brown hair curled on her shoulders; she wore colorful scarves and slanted hats.

When she played the piano, we watched her fan her skirt, making sure the pleats were even and falling a half circle from the back of the bench. She never played the pieces from beginning to end, and though the music was choppy, it cheered up the old house.

Sometimes, she paused in the middle of a piece and laughed—a long, slow laugh that endured like lines of smooth piano chords—and we believed at that moment she was where she wanted to be, wherever that might have been.

Salad Garden

The waiter stumbled from the restaurant where he had worked for fifteen years. Without warning, the owner, Don Carlos, had fired him. The finality of that sentence fell on him like stones. The highest volcano in Mexico could have erupted and it would not have equaled the impact of this fate. He had kept a straight line by working, without a routine he could fall into a rut.

Each step toward his small house, toward his wife and their child, down the dusty path to the *barrio* where they lived, became heavier. Here he was, a stupid little man in canvas shoes, white cotton pants and black serving jacket. He had made the salads at the restaurant, was known to blend a perfect Caesar dressing and had hopes that one day he'd be a real waiter. Now he was nothing.

That day, the mayor came to lunch with a businessman. Right away, they got into an argument. Don Carlos, the owner, sensing tension, offered them Cuban rum. They drank one and then another and then more before the waiter wheeled the salad cart to their table. A gun bulged under the businessman's coat, his nose was blue, red lines spidered in his cheeks, he tapped cigar ash onto the floor. He kept looking at the door as if he expected someone to arrive that he did not want to see. He and the mayor paid no attention as the waiter mixed in oil and vinegar, anchovies, parsley, an egg and cheese and then tossed in the lettuce. Their argument mounted, something about a payoff, a road contract that the businessman wanted from the mayor. The mayor hesitated, shook his head, mentioned prior commitments, a lack of funds, that the timing was not in favor of this project.

The salad maker listened as he whisked the egg, thinking that with the flavor of his sauce, he could turn their dispute around. Eating the salad would make them forget. It had happened; the blending of ingredients—fresh lettuce grown in Don Carlos's ranchito, anchovies from the coast and cheese imported from a distant country made people content.

But he was wrong. The businessman and the mayor had not even touched the salad before the businessman rose from the table, flipped his plate, yelled at the mayor, tripped on his chair, and rushed off. Don Carlos ran to the mayor. The mayor blamed the salad and told Don Carlos to get rid of the wormy salad maker or he'd take his business elsewhere, and furthermore, he never liked the looks of that pockmarked, stooped, smiling, bowing server.

Without work, the salad maker's old enemy—mescal—tempted him until all he could think about was getting drunk. He gave up looking for a job, slept all day, threw things against the wall and pushed his wife and child. At night, he crept around the *barrio*, begging for spirits—the thick, sour fermented alcohol blurred the edges for a while, until blackouts and splitting headaches came. Each hour somehow began and ended, until one afternoon he returned to find his wife and child gone.

He staggered beyond the city and then through fields, thinking he'd find them at her sister's village, but he got lost. He slept in a clearing; owls hooted, dogs barked, dew fell. He woke to a swollen tongue and emptiness. He woke rumpled and shaking and hungry as if he had slept for a night, a day and another night. Yet, through the mist he saw in front of him each salad he'd ever made, arranged in rows like heads of lettuce in a vegetable garden. The green leaves reminded him of the pungent smell of oil in the teak bowl, the feel of the salad forks in his hands, and the reassuring clink of wheels of the cart as he pushed it over the terracotta tiles.

He stood to go to the salad garden, to touch one of his creations, but the garden was just out of reach, and he was exhausted. His legs buckled. Sun burned through the mist, he closed his eyes and fell into thinking how every day he had put on his serving jacket. Every day he had stood in front of the little mirror in their house and tied his tie. Every day he had walked up to the restaurant to do what he liked best. Then he thought about the jacket, the pockets, the worn collar, about fastening the plastic black buttons, and how the jacket was still there, hanging on the nail behind the door, waiting.

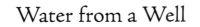
Water from a Well

Imagine a film in soft color focusing on an elegant Mexican woman spending a typical day in her house. She lives with me—her only child—on a cobblestone street in the colonial neighborhood of San Angel outside of Mexico City. It is the 1950s; her hair is short and curled at her neck; she wears twill skirts, white blouses and low heels. She's navigating around the rooms; pours water into plants on the kitchen windowsill, shows a new maid how to blend chilies and tomatoes for an enchilada sauce, braids my hair, ties the sash of my dress, sits in a tall chair at her desk writing letters to friends she met at a finishing school in London. She picks marguerite daisies in the garden, lies in the shade under the trellis reading Pablo Neruda, or on rainy days sinks into the couch by the fire.

Imagine her every morning drawing a simple image in her sketching diary—bougainvillea viewed from her bedroom window, curved shadow of a broom against a wall, leafy reflections in the birdbath, my hands holding a picture book. Imagine her rubbing cold cream onto her thin fingers, rubbing my back at bedtime, standing in the breeze at a doorway rubbing her arms from a chill.

Now the film is grainy black and white. It is the late sixties, and I've come bursting back from the first of the student demonstrations at the university campus south of Mexico City. I am embarrassed by our wealth and do not bring new friends to our colonial house. I ignore my mother's questions about where I go. I am fascinated that Trotsky lived in our neighborhood. I reprimand my mother for being conservative, skeptical of feminism, for having maids and a gardener. I tell her she lacks courage and is a lonely, secretive widow who floats within the security of her world. I lecture her about capitalism exploiting Indians. I cut her off when she responds—her point of view is out of date. My hair is long, straight. I wear embroidered Mexican blouses over baggy jeans and huarache sandals like a migrant worker. When I look in the mirror, I do not see the adored child I was. I wonder how I might have resembled my deceased Spanish father. I go to live with friends of our family in Los Angeles but am lonely in their house—everything is white, the television always on. In America, I feel like a Mexicana, a second-class citizen. I miss smells of mesquite burning in fireplaces, tortillas on the griddle, jasmine. I yearn for days when my mother read me her favorite stories.

Muted, bleached color bleeds back into the film. Seven years later, the camera is seeing us from above. My mother is ill from the hereditary cancer that took her mother. I've finished my Master degree in Latin American Studies at UCLA and am back in Mexico to stay. My mother is lying on the couch. Like a child. I want to pick her up, but I'm afraid she'll dissolve if I touch her. Her voice is thin, a whisper. Afternoon fades. It is then, in the gray evening light, she tells me I am not her biological daughter. She says she did not inform me before because she did not want me to feel unloved, adopted. Now she knows I must know the truth. My father had had a relationship with a maid. My mother feels blessed to have me. With this new information, I can only observe her—there are no words yet. Her cheeks are transparent, milky. Waves of brown hair frame her face, her green eyes. I feel thick and dark. We do not share blood, veins or genes. My father died when I was four. My real mother is somewhere—in a house caring for old people, in the countryside carrying kindling, in a village hauling buckets of water from a well.

The Reader

As a blind woman of thirty-two, Luisa had solved the problem of lonely evenings. During weeknights, at seven, the doorbell rang; the maid opened it and let Antonio in.

"*Buenas tardes,*" he called out. "I'll be right there." She heard him in the kitchen, knocking around in the cupboard for a bottle of wine, saying something to Rosa, popping the cork, and then she heard the clinking of glasses on the tray. She tuned the radio to a classical station. He leaned against the swinging door and came into the sitting room.

"Right on time," she said, relieved for the company. She wondered what he was thinking when he came to her house. A spoiled woman needing help? That it was odd to see someone just sitting? Could he sense who she was?

Antonio set the tray on the coffee table, put his canvas satchel on the floor and took out newspapers and magazines he'd bought at a newsstand. He'd been reading to her for a few weeks.

"To another cool evening," he said as he handed her a glass.

"I wish I could say I know that. I've not been out in a while, not even on the terrace." Luisa smiled, but was not sure he was looking at her.

Antonio had grown up on a cattle *estancia* in Argentina. For an adventure he had come to work on a family friend's ranch in Sinaloa, quit (said the cattle were not well cared for), and now claimed he was content doing odd jobs in Mexico City until his planned return to South America in the winter. He mentioned, when she interviewed him on the phone, that he liked books, and that when he was a child, his father had read to the family in the evenings.

Though she could not see him—since the car crash last year, she could only make out blurry shapes—she sensed he was tall and imagined he was strong and good-looking in an Italian way, like many Argentine men. His presence made her feel lighter and more talkative than usual. There was something safe in discussing politics or art with someone who was hired and, in his case, would be around only for a few months.

As he read magazine stories and articles his voice was confident and lively, though once he stumbled onto a short poem by the famous Mexican poet, Sor Juana and said, "I can't relate. Poetry's a puzzle." He had other opinions Luisa found provincial: Mexican painters were abstract, the recent—early 1980s—residential architecture was boxy and bland, he didn't understand why children were allowed to beg or why a country with agriculture, coasts, and Spanish heritage had so many poor people. It was as if he had never known of his own roots, his own country where there were beggars, coasts and the pampas full of wheat and hay.

Yet, after a week or so, Luisa felt something inside of her soften. His voice soothed her, and she woke up many mornings impatient for the day to pass. She wanted to touch his face, to feel his whiskers on her palm, outline his nose with her finger, hold his face in both hands. But instead—blushing, becoming shy with these yearnings and this new need to see tactically—she leaned her head back and listened to him read.

"You look great," Antonio said one evening. His voice was polite, measured. She blushed and said, *"Gracias,"* but felt a lump in her throat. She often tried to imagine what she did look like. A thin woman wearing tinted glasses at night. Short brown hair lifting from her neck in the breeze of an open window. Pale complexion now that she was no longer hiking in the countryside. Were her fingernails clean? The scar on her forehead? It was strange not to know. It was strange to have a whole new inner world whirl in her mind. One that no one else could see, would care about, could understand. She lived with shadows within the blurriness of her cloudy vision, with thoughts that never before came to mind, dreams where she wandered, fled, ran into walls, woke up in a sweat, woke up in perpetual darkness, dreams that did not offer anything about a hopeful future, dreams that ended up with a black night, no dawn, no daylight.

But she knew how she felt. She swayed in a constant dislocation of not seeing, in a lingering confusion. There was the silent lonely adjustment to a small dark world. There were the early days when she did not sleep, in her fear of the dark, in fear of the moment color would drain from her dreams. Then there was that voice in her, tempting her to give up, to fall down the stairs, to swallow all the medication, to step into a busy intersection. Her struggle back, her swimming upstream in a strong current, running from rain in the monsoon; she had been breathless, jittery. She could feel her friends backing away, as if tiptoeing, afraid of her neediness. But then something shifted: sun on her skin, whiffs of cut grass, lemon in tea, rain, fires on cold days, the next chord in a guitar concerto.

Luisa proofed young-adult books on tape. At least it was work. A few months ago she moved to Mexico City to make a life for herself somehow. For the last five years she had lived in southern Mexico, in Oaxaca, where she charted ancient Mayan trails for a map company. Now she was here—perhaps forever—in her grandmother's house she had inherited.

"Are you happy, Luisa? I mean okay? It'd be good for you to get out and walk. Have you thought about a guide dog?" Antonio asked her one night. It was the first time he spoke directly about her blindness. The first time he stepped over the line of just being a reader.

She looked down. His suggestion stung. They sat in silence. He did not commence reading; he waited. The clock ticked. She might at least have said she was getting used to being blind, finding her way. But about a dog, she could not answer him.

Nine years ago, Luisa started off from where she parked her car above Mexico City in the national park, El Desierto de los Leones. The sack she carried clawed her shoulder. Below her the city simmered in the late afternoon fog, which was really smog—but no one in the 1970s wanted to call the cloud cover by its correct name. She stood by a mesquite tree and adjusted the strap so the weight was evenly distributed across her thin shoulder blades. The sack was limp, a dead weight that landed on her hip—the weight of a dead dog.

She heard bells. A church, a chapel? She wasn't sure. She pictured people gathering—women in shawls, factory workers, beggars, veiled women shuffling through the large wooden doors that were now open, luring them to Mass.

The terrain at the base of the mountain was rough with jutting rocks and scraggly bushes. A path that she'd once been on with her grandparents wound its way to the ruin of a monastery before giving way to the grassy slopes above tree line. The cave-like cells of the monastery used to be open for visitors. At that time a blind monk sold candles at the entrance. The monk's eyes were droopy, and when he held his hand out to take the money, she noticed that his eyeballs were glassy white. Now Luisa avoided walking near the crumbling building even though it had been closed long ago. She never forgot the monk, and suddenly remembered how he had appeared off and on for years in her dreams, where he struck one match after another, trying to light a candle, but the flame extinguished before he could find the wick.

The path left the collapsed rooftops of the monastery behind. As a first-year student, she had grown used to carrying her backpack of books from class to class at the University in Mexico City; it was balanced at least, but the awkwardness of this sack made it tricky to walk over rocks. After an hour or so the trail opened up, the air freshened and became cooler. Warm from walking, Luisa pulled her scarf loose from her neck and paused when she heard the trickle of a stream. Sounds of the city and the bells were now quieted. The grass, burned from relentless sun, crackled under foot. Finally, she set the sack down. Lightheaded, she shielded her eyes from the glare and scanned the slope looking for the stream. She was buying time, she knew that, but then again, what was the rush? The cooler air filled her with renewed energy. She was beginning to feel strong enough to do her task.

Presently, she felt someone was watching. Or had followed her. She thought of the blind monk. No one was around. Just the dog. It was the presence of the dog she sensed. The dead dog in the sack. She opened the sack and looked inside. She lowered her hand onto the dog to touch it. His coat was scratchy, skin stretched over bony ribs. She pulled him out with both hands and placed him on the grass. His neck hung slack, broken, the tail between his legs, curled, stiff. He was beginning to smell from being in the sack. This was the first time she had looked at him since she had found him on the street at noon. He was a brown and white spotted mutt—one of thousands of dogs that get run over or starve in Mexico every day—that had probably survived this long by sniffing for garbage, sleeping in the shade of wrecked cars, and running from boys throwing stones.

When she saw the dead dog, there was a pang. She scooped him from the gutter and placed him in a sack she had in her backpack. It was what she had to do. It was a way to pay.

Now, on the Desierto, she sat down by the dog and thought again about the stream. The sound was pleasant, with water rattling small rocks. It calmed her. In a way, she felt she had accomplished so much that it was good to stop for a moment. She'd look around later, when she was finished. She took out the trowel borrowed from her grandparents' garden shed and considered where to place the grave. Maybe over there, under the only tree? She surprised herself, thinking that it mattered where she buried him. But if it had been the other dog—her own dog, her beloved childhood dog—she would bury him where she would have liked to be buried, with a view, in the center of the hillside. She laughed in a burst of confused emotion. She stood up and for no good reason began to dig where her feet had flattened tufts of grass. The earth was hard, but in a while she managed to make a hole. She yanked her scarf off, beads of sweat pooled on her lip, blisters formed on her fingers. She worked without looking at the dog, but was distracted by the buzz of flies and looked quickly at his face where saliva had dried and matted the whiskers. His mouth had shrunken, exposing his teeth. When the hole was just big enough, she lifted him into it and scooped the dirt back over his body. The flies flew off. If he had been her dog, she'd want him close to the surface, not buried under stones and layers of chalky dirt. With a flat hand she patted the grave. Then she stood up, clapped the dirt from her hands, put the trowel in the sack and backed away from the mound she'd made. Thoughts of her old dog came to mind— her old dog who must have roamed the streets after she had left him in Lima—that dog panting, sniffing, always hopeful, still looking for her.

"It will be a blessing for him," her father had announced one day at breakfast. She was fifteen. They were moving from Lima to London for another four-year tour for his job in the embassy before returning to Mexico. "It's not humane to keep a dog in quarantine. It'll be best to put Paco to sleep. He's old. He won't know the difference."

But for Luisa that could never happen.

Luisa lied to her parents and told them that a friend would adopt her dog, but none of her friends liked dogs. A few days before they left, she walked the dog through Lima past a working class *barrio* to the beach where strays roamed, beggars slept along the ramparts, children flew kites, and where there was garbage. Paco charged off, free to chase shadows of sea gulls. She watched him bound away, his terrier legs propelling him. The blood drained from her face. She felt rubbery, her heart hammered in her chest, but, as she knew she had to do, she turned and ran. Someone would love him, someone would feed him was all she could allow herself to think. He had wandered into her life; he could wander into someone else's.

"Well," Antonio said, "I guess I'll be going. Your mind is elsewhere."

Luisa flinched.

"Wait," she said, "don't leave." She heard him folding the newspaper. She feared it was too late; he would not wait for what she wanted to say. She didn't know what she had to say, but she wanted to say something, to explain it all.

What she knew was that she had a bad sense of timing sometimes, except last year in that one instant of precision when she swerved her car. Then, after that swerve, she lost control, skidded through the corner and careened off into the tree. What was it? She was not sure, but, as the car veered off the road—in what seemed oddly like slow motion—she saw out of the corner of her eye an animal, a dog, run into the bushes.

Luisa put down her glass, stood up and said, "how about we take a walk."

Scent

Marina woke up in a hotel in the little town of Careyes on the Pacific Ocean in Mexico. She was attending a writers' workshop. It was Friday. The classes were to begin Saturday afternoon. She rolled onto her back and observed the room, the simplicity of the four white walls. The quiet, the stillness of the morning, made her self-aware. She realized that in time, with marriage and children, she had lost track of who she had become. Now a presence filled her like air in an old house.

It was an odd feeling, this self-consciousness. As she got up to pull the curtains open, she was aware of each limb moving independently: her nightgown against her leg, her ankle, her toe curled on the tile floor. She could feel the pulse in her temples. Reaching up to the curtain, she saw her hand by itself, as if it were an infant's hand stretching for a toy it could not quite reach. This hand, which had been automatically employed to do motherly tasks, now appeared vulnerable and alone—the thin fingers, the nails, the plain wedding band, the skin covering blue veins suspended, as if caught doing something wrong. She observed it for a moment. What if? What if she couldn't complete the task? What if her hand began to choose its own movements? What if she became paralyzed and would have to depend on someone else to open the curtain—or leave it shut forever?

The thought scared her. She threw back the muslin panels and looked at the beach. Waves lapped the sand. Low clouds stretched along the horizon, overhead the sky was blue. Hotel men were setting chairs under the palm trees. She wasn't sure how long she had thought about this moment when she would be on the beach, where she could write in peace; it seemed strange that it was finally happening now. She had derived such refuge in the dream of a time for herself.

The hotel beach was in a cove. Waves brought strands of seaweed onto the hard-packed gray sand. She found a chair and a small table and set down her notebook and tube of sun cream. She had planned to walk along the shore every morning to clear her thoughts and have a clean slate for writing. Now that urge was gone. A surge of disappointment spilled, like a child who comes home after a long trip to find her house smaller, and rooms once bright, now dull.

In this diminished reality, it seemed suddenly wrong to have come at all. She leaned back in the chair and looked at the sky. A breeze gave her the chills. Reaching for her shirt, she noticed an older man walking toward her.

The man introduced himself as Carlo Antoniori. He was the Italian owner of the hotel. Though in his sixties, he looked strong and healthy. A mustache made him appear more Mexican than Italian. He was wearing khaki pants, a white shirt with sleeves rolled up and espadrilles. Marina was drawn to the brightness in his blue eyes.

"I'm sorry to have bothered your solitude. I thought you were someone else."

Marina looked up at him, blocking the sun with her hand. Carlo shifted his stance to stand in front of the glare.

She introduced herself, asked about the weather, laughed and said, "What a question. I guess it's always pleasant here."

Carlo smiled and said, "Yes, it is always agreeable here. Even if it rains. If you have no plans later, if you're up for seeing a bird refuge, I'm going this afternoon to check on a duck nest. It's on a salt pond nestled between the sea and a coastal hill—it's beautiful. I often invite guests to join me."

Hours later, Marina was sitting next to him in an old Jeep rattling down a dirt road. She sat in the bouncing car, trying to keep herself from being thrown toward him. She was glad for an outing. Carlo was concentrating on navigating around the potholes.

"You see," Carlo said, as if continuing an ongoing conversation, "I was spiritually dying in Italy. After the war, everyone wore black. Then came the student riots in France. My life was running out. I was sad. I became restless. I wanted life to be special. I did not want to work in our family bank."

Marina turned to look at him, but he stopped his train of thought as abruptly as he had begun. The road dipped down a hill and then crossed a streambed. Water sprayed on Marina's arm resting on the door. Carlo continued.

"I had a dream about Mexico. I'd never been here, but I dreamt I fell in love with the sensuality of this country." He was staring ahead, concentrating, his left wrist on the steering wheel.

"What do you mean?"

"In my dream I awoke to the pleasures of smell. When a man loves a woman, it's for her scent. I wanted a life where there would be fragrance in the air."

Carlo stopped the car and turned off the engine. He kicked open the door, got out, walked to a bush, pulled off a branch and brought it over to Marina's side of the car.

"Smell this," he said as he handed her the branch. Marina held it in front of her nose and inhaled, but she couldn't smell anything.

"It's subtle. Allow the scent in," Carlo said.

She felt like laughing.

"Think how pure the leaves are. They have a flavor. Close your eyes."

Marina found herself obeying. When she closed her eyes the fragrance came to her. It was faint, a bit like sage, but bitter.

"Now I smell it," she said. "I never would've noticed."

Carlo jumped back in the car, started the engine, and they drove on. Marina held onto the branch and noticed that the scent came and went, but she wasn't able to hold on to it long enough to memorize it.

They arrived at a stretch of road that burrowed through an overgrown patch of dense manzanilla. She copied Carlo when he rolled up his window. Even though he was driving slowly, the branches clawed the car doors and scratched the roof like fingernails. Marina ducked. They came to a little clearing, and once again Carlo stopped the car and turned it off. He rolled down his window and told her to do the same.

"Now listen," he whispered. "We might be lucky, but we have to be quiet."

Marina didn't dare ask what they were listening for. Carlo was completely still. A part of him had disappeared, as if his personality had slipped away from his body like a mystic in a trance. She strained her ears. Thoughts clashed. She tried clearing her mind, but rather than finding peace, there was anxiety. Fleeting images of her family and her life in their house in Ohio came to mind. She saw herself walking away from them in the airport, her skirt swaying. Now that memory seemed far away.

Carlo's eyes were glued to the thicket in front of them. Marina sensed not to move. She wanted to slip out of her sneakers and cross her legs. She wanted to put the branch on the seat. Her face itched. She began to feel angry. The old feeling of being manipulated into behaving a certain way so that a man's needs could be met came to her. Yet here, Carlo was not asking for anything. He was absorbed in expectation. He had invited her along to show her something.

A faint breeze made its way to them, barely stirring the manzanilla. Marina turned to Carlo. He looked like a boy. His face flushed, his expression alert, his eyes wide open. Suddenly he raised his eyebrows, a smile broke his trance. He lifted his chin to indicate something was happening. Marina saw a rustle in the undergrowth. A family of possums scampered across the road. The babies were like puppies, jumping in excitement. They paused in the road, played for a moment and then disappeared under the brush, leaving tracks in the powdery soil.

"We were lucky to see them," Carlo beamed. "They're nocturnal."

Marina sighed. And they're shy, she thought. They drove the rest of the way through the thicket and arrived at the salt pond.

"We have to walk from here," Carlo said. Reeds and cattails surrounded the pond. The water was brackish and smelled like fish. Birds were taking flight and landing, stirring the surface. Carlo took off his espadrilles and carried them. They walked inland a few moments, following a path through the reeds. With each step, the soggy ground sucked Marina's sneakers from her feet, causing her to fall behind. She couldn't see which way he went. The path narrowed, the reeds were dense. She stopped and wondered where to go. There was no breeze, she felt light-headed, her legs were heavy. What if she stepped into quick-sand? Or was bitten by a snake?

A birdsong pierced the heat. She turned to look for the bird and saw a clearing in the path. Ahead, she could see Carlo waiting by the pond's edge.

When she reached him, he said, "I found this for you." He pressed a shell into her palm and cupped her hand with his. He stared into her eyes. His expression burned into her embarrassment. She tried to release her hand from his grip, but he held it tight.

"Keep this shell," he said.

She dared to look at him directly. When their eyes met, she smiled.

"Conch shells sound like the sea. This scallop shell is silent. Listen for silence. That's where wisdom dwells." He let go of her hand and took two steps backwards.

"Now come along. I want to see if the duck nest is still in the thicket over there."

He turned to walk up the path. A gull flew low, skimmed the brush and then glided toward the sea. The shell, small as her thumbnail, was warm against her skin and fit in the deepest part of her palm.

A moment later he said, "It's here. I was afraid an eagle might have stolen the eggs, but they're still here."

Marina caught up and peered into the nest. They stood for a while as if expecting the eggs to hatch, until Carlo looked in the direction of the setting sun and said, "We must go."

On the way back, Carlo paused at the possum crossing and pointed to the meandering path the possums had made in the road. He leaned out of the car for a moment, then shifted gears and accelerated.

Marina looked at him. His eyes were lively, darting to the left and right, looking for the next animal or bird. As the road rose and fell through the scrub forest and streambeds, Marina ran her thumb over the fluted back of the shell—did *it* smell like something? The sea, salt, a mollusk? Or was it free of its scent, free of its past?

Dede Reed is a writer and photographer who lived in Mexico in the 1980s.

Made in the USA
Middletown, DE
25 November 2019